THE SPACEMAN

And other stories and poems

W. B. EDWARDS

Table of Contents

Thank you, dear reader, for purchasing this small volume!

While edited for grammatical errors and spelling, most of these stories and poems were written during the 1960s and '70s, and I have not changed them. *Jesus Ramirez* for instance, was written for my first Creative Writing class sometime in 1966 or '67. Rio Hondo was a Junior College in those days, and the brand-new campus in 1966 seemed fantastic to this young high school grad. I decided to major in Liberal Arts and of course, signed up for Creative Writing. The instructor was a fellow named William Burns, who resembled the actor Richard Burton, who inspired his students to write whatever they truly wanted, but also to try writing things we didn't, such as poetry, in my case. Mainly, he told us to write, write, write! And he had literary connections. At least twice during the two years I attended, he managed to have Ray Bradbury speak to our class. I do wish my memory was better, as I'm sure I'm forgetting other Authors whom he may have conjured for our edification.

While attending Rio Hondo, I also took Journalism classes for a few semesters, and regret to this day that I didn't pursue it further. I remember I found it boring. While I wanted to be the next Hemingway, I failed to realize how much journalism had influenced my hero's craft. Well, I have many regrets these days.

But those college days were filled with fun and discovery. It was the Sixties, after all. *Sergeant Pepper, Ravi Shankar, The Graduate, Simon and Garfunkel.* Because I had several friends in Creative Writing who were also studying Drama, I got to hang out with all the Drama folks in the coffee shop on campus, where we smoked too many cigarettes and discussed world politics. One fine Jewish fellow I remember, Bob something, felt so strongly about the events happening in Israel that he joined the Israeli Army to fight in what became known as the *Seven Day War*. Sadly, we never saw him again. Another vivid memory I have is attending the college's stage production of *A Mid Summer's Night Dream* with my then fiancé, where we chatted with a very kind and affable *Burgess Meredith* as we waited in the queue outside. I don't know what happened to any of the people I knew at college, but they live on in my memories, hazy as they might be. Sometime in the mid-80s I returned to visit the campus and didn't see anything or anyone I recognized. Such is life.

Anyway, the old saying tells us that 'you can't go home again', but writers can, and often do. And hopefully, we can bring anyone along who wants to go with us.

THE ROADSIDE DINER

Outside the rain fell steadily from the cold gray desert sky, fogging the glass windows, but the red and green neon letters that said *Joe's Roadside Diner* was bright enough when lit up and flashing that any passerby on the lonely two-lane highway could easily spot the place. Joe could see it was still very dark outside and the sound of the rain on the slanted roof was as loud and insistent as the non-existent traffic had once been. He finished making the day's first pot of coffee, and pouring out a cup for his wife, hurried to carry it out back into their living quarters.

"Morning time, Mona," he said.

Mona turned over in the bed with a sigh, her long brown hair spreading over the white pillow, looking up at him with a bright smile.

"You brought me coffee?" she said as if surprised. It was their daily ritual and had been for nearly thirty years.

"Yes, dear."

"Is it still raining?"

"Yes, dear."

Joe placed the cup into Mona's outstretched hands and still nodding at her as she hummed sweetly at him, turned from the bed to head back out to the diner. It was not yet time to open.

Yes, it was too early to open, but Joe and his wife both liked rising early to savor the quiet before the desert dawn. Outside the rain seemed to be softening.

Mona came out into the diner looking as soft and happy as a warm kitten in her dark brown robe and gave her husband a little kiss on his stubbled cheek.

"What time is it, anyway?" she said.

" 'Bout five-thirty," said Joe, not looking at the clock on the wall over the register behind them.

"I wonder when all this rain will stop. How many days has it been now?"

"Only three days, off and on. It's that time of year out here. It'll stop soon enough."

Joe poured a cup for himself and sat next to his wife at the counter. They sat on the round backless stools with their backs to the counter, looking out at the darkness.

"Probably be even slower than usual today," Mona said after a while.

"Always slow on Sundays," said Joe.

"Hmm."

"Mona?"

"Hmm. Yeah."

"I've been thinking."

"About what?"

"Maybe we ought to just stay closed on Sundays."

"Won't be any easier now than it was before, money-wise. We tried that, remember?"

"Yeah. But we don't even clear twenty bucks most Sundays."

"Twenty bucks is twenty bucks."

"Hardly pays the bills."

"Well, it helps."

"I don't know, Joe. We could drive over to town and go to church or something instead. Take a drive in the mountains afterward. Or have lunch in the city."

They sipped their coffee, watching as a tinge of gray began to grow in the darkness outside. Then they saw that two men were standing outside, watching them through the foggy glass.

Joe stood and walked over to the front doors and after unlocking it, opened it a crack, feeling the cold wind hit him in the face. "We're not ready to open yet," he called out to the men. "Half an hour to go."

"Please, mister! It's damn cold out here!" a young voice pleaded.

Joe looked back at Mona, who slowly nodded her assent.

The two men turned out to be teenaged boys, probably no older than seventeen years, Joe guessed. They were not local kids. One was taller and skinnier than the other, who was too heavy looking for his age. The taller boy's face was pockmarked with angry red acne scars and the shorter boy had two small sad-looking eyes set deep in his doughy looking white skin. They both stared at Mona as they came in before taking seats at the counter.

"We need some hot coffee. You got any donuts?" said the skinny kid.

Joe walked around behind his counter and putting a smile on his face, poured out two cups of coffee and set them in front of the boys. Then he laid out napkins and spoons and forks. "What kind of donuts would you like?" he asked. "We could scramble up some eggs and toast for ya, ya know? Some real food."

"Chocolate," said the shorter boy.

"Yeah, some eggs sound real good," said the skinny boy.

"We ain't got enough money for a big breakfast," said the fat boy.

"Shut the fuck up," said the skinny boy.

"Sure, Mike, I'm just..."

"Shut up!"

"But you said we should..."

"You're so fucking stupid, man."

Joe heard this but pretended he didn't, setting out two saucer-sized plates with the last of yesterday's donuts in front of the boys. It just so happened they were chocolate glazed donuts. "Here ya go, boys," he said. "And they're on the house since we don't have any fresh ones until tomorrow." He grinned at the boys.

"Ya got any cream?" asked the boy named Mike.

"Sure," said Joe, turning to the cold case behind him. Mike poured a small amount into his coffee, which his friend quickly repeated.

Mona had been sitting silently, sipping her coffee and watching the dawn light spread across the gray sky outside. Now she finished her coffee and rising quietly, nodded at her husband before heading out through the doors through the kitchen towards their rooms in the back.

"Where you boys headed?" said Joe.

"California," said the shorter boy.

Mike looked as if he wanted to sneeze or something.

"We don't usually open this early on Sundays, but you boys looked pretty cold and wet out there. Where's your car, anyway? Are you hiking across this desert?"

"What're these forks for?" said Mike, making the other boy snigger.

"Some people want them, even for donuts and such," said Joe.

The boy sniggered again, and Mike told him to keep quiet.

"It's okay," said Joe good-naturedly.

"I was just asking what the fork was for."

"Well, it's also a kind of habit, putting them out when people sit down."

"You have any more?" asked the shorter kid.

"No sir, no more donuts until tomorrow. How about some toast and jam?"

"You don't need another damn donut, fatty," said Mike.

"Well, as long as you got no more chocolates, I guess I don't want one anyway."

"How about some more coffee, then," said Joe.

"Sure," said both boys together.

Joe filled their cups, leaving the cream on the counter. "I'm going out back for a second," he told them. "Don't get lost."

When he was gone Mike turned to his friend. "You wanna get laid?"

"What?"

"You're so lame, man. We can screw that lady."

"What lady?"

"Jesus."

"Mike, I'm sorry, I don't remember any lady. Oh, wait..."

"Well, do you wanna? Did you see how she was sitting over there, with nuthin' on under that robe? Man, nice boobs for an old lady!"

"Oh yeah, I remember. Sure, I do!"

"Well, do you want to? Gotta decide now, man."

"Yeah, I guess..."

"Get off your ass then and go grab that big black skillet over there and get behind the door. When that dude comes out hit him right over his head, hard as you can. Can you do that, fatty?"

"Okay Mike, I will."

When Joe came back through the kitchen doorway he was smiling, but Fatty hit him over his head from behind and his smile and his world crumpled to the floor. Mona came out of the door and began screaming, causing Mike to jump up quickly, barely preventing his friend from smashing her head in as well. Mike grabbed her arms and began trying to push her down, trying to get her on the floor behind the counter.

"You bastards!" she screamed, again and again, twisting wildly in his grip. But Mike was taller and stronger than Mona and soon they had her on the floor, tearing off her clothes and pushing her bra up towards her neck. Mike straddled her, while the other boy held her arms, stretching them high and putting his knees on her shoulders. Mona passed out, then jerked awake again when she began choking on her vomit and the boy put both his palms over her mouth, breaking her jaw, and she soon passed out again.

When Mike was finished, he stood quickly and zipped up his jeans. "Let's go," he said. "Let's get the money and get outta here. And turn off the fucking lights, man! Are you an idiot?"

"What about me?" said the other boy.

"Forget it, fatty. Not much good, anyway."

Outside the rain had stopped, but there was still a heavy mist falling and the clouds were dark and heavy with rain. A few cars and trucks drove past on the highway, but the diner's lights were cold and nobody stopped. Finally, a policeman on his way home from patrol pulled in, wanting something hot on such a cold morning. A regular customer, he knew Joe and Mona and realized something must be wrong when he didn't see the familiar red neon lights, but he didn't know just how terribly wrong it was going to be until he went inside.

They never lose

Oh yes
here we are
all alone
looking closely
or staring far
oh yes
here we are
we move
we groove
we shake our heads
laugh at them
oh yeah
we do
but
they never lose.
Oh yes
here we are
all alone
and we wait
alone or together
we breathe
or we hold our breath
are we all
scared of them?

Yes we are
'cause they never lose.
Oh yes
here we are
we move
we groove
we see what comes
and stick our heads
in the ground
'cause nothing good
ever comes around
oh yes
we laugh at them
But they never lose!

#1

Going down nightly
Slipping down slightly
It's Soft
Softness now prevails
Even a soft cry
Floats away
Sailing
On bright, tiny crystals
In soft blue seas
Bound for a soft, smooth
Liquid blue infinity

FAR UP CREEK

So, far up creek
and near downstream
(tries so hard to be a dream)
Bitter nights and cold, cold days
sunken dreams
float away
Salty faces hasten
looking benign
(summer moon fall all shine)
I slip my boats
to float my lakes
For bitter nights, and colder days
For hot ice cream, and cold, cold cakes
Tangerine ladies, so far out wide
(winter moon spring all slide)
They're all so full, nothing with inside
a little bit more, and a whole lot less
only circles turn
(children guess)
None from some
I gained my loss
(wind moon rain all tossed)
Finally found my new forgot
where some things

only crave about
and only spins
the circle stop
So far up creek
And near downstream
(it tried only like a dream)
A warmer night froze one day
And I whiled my happy dazed away

VICTOR'S VICTORY

The morning came and Victor woke up lying crookedly in the twisted cockpit of his small airplane with the sun in his eyes, blinding him. He sat up to look around and saw the desert, all golden and warm and fresh in the dawn light. He sighed at the memory of the night before and then climbed out of the wreckage of his small plane.

One of the wings was badly smashed and bent, as was the single propeller and nose. He had come in and nosed over, catching the wing on the uneven ground. It was his fault, and he knew it beyond any doubt. What would Angie say? He knew he should have checked the fuel, but he had been in too big a hurry to get airborne and away from his wife. And he shouldn't have flown out over this area, not at night. Sam had warned him before. Now he was lost, he thought. No air traffic in this area. Of course, they'd send search planes or helicopters, but what chance would there be of spotting his little brown plane out here? Very little.

He thought of the night before, trying to remember the details. He had flown nearly due east for almost two hours before the engine began to sputter, scaring the hell out of him. He thought he'd seen lights below, maybe a highway or one of those desolate missile bases that were supposed to be out here. But he had no idea how far back those lights were, too much had happened just getting the plane down on her belly. But there was a chance he could go back and find something resembling civilization and that chance left no choice: he would have to walk. Maybe it wouldn't be too far. Since there was nothing inside the plane to take with him, Victor turned his back on the little plane and began walking before remembering the radio. He ran back to the plane, a huge smile on his face. But the radio was smashed. Damn, he said aloud. He started again, walking as best he could judge from the sun, directly towards the west.

Ahead were low hills and beyond the hills dark, distant mountains. There was also a small conical-looking mountain rising from the midst of the low hills. Out there, somewhere, he thought, is safety. At least he hoped so.

After a mile or so he decided it was not too bad walking in the desert. The sun was not too strong, and it felt cool enough. He wished he was wearing better shoes or some boots. Tennis shoes, he decided, weren't made for walking in the desert. They were making his feet sweat. Then he remembered he needed to watch for snakes. And spiders, he thought. He'd always been afraid of spiders.

He knew Angie would be angry he'd crashed the plane. They'd paid a lot of money for it. Against her wishes, at least until she found out Sam and Alicia were buying one. Then she changed her tune. And he didn't think she'd be very worried, not for real anyway, but she'd pretend for the sake of appearances. That's the way she was. But so what? What could she do to him out here? He laughed a little, and his situation seemed lighter. It was a little fun even. An adventure. He would come out of this unscathed. Sunburnt and weary, but alive and a better man for it. Victor smiled. When he got home Sam, and all the others would recognize the change in him. They would see his sunburned face and his weary, dried-out body, but they would also see his knowing smile, a smile of victory. They would see a new man. And Angie would be forced to see it too, she would have to smile proudly and go along with the others. It will be like a new role for her, he thought. He almost wanted to kick himself for not doing this sooner.

After two hours the sun became really hot, beating down. His head and armpits itched with sweat. He took off his blue jacket and put it over his head like an Arab. He was Lawrence of Arabia. He'd crossed several of the little hills already but had seen nothing, none of them were high enough to see very far. Once he'd turned around and looked back but he couldn't see the little airplane either. The distant mountains were no longer dark, but brown and ugly and seemed no closer. The only thing closer was the little mountain that resembled an ice cream cone turned upside down. Victor walked and walked, and it seemed there would never be an end to the walking before he reached that big cone or anything else.

Victor began to realize he was getting very thirsty, and hungry too. His feet were beginning to hurt badly. He wished clouds would come and hide the sun.

He thought of his wife again. Angie. Angelina. But she wasn't an angel, no she wasn't. What about that Pro at the country club? Victor had known about it all along but had preferred to leave it alone. He wondered if she knew that he knew. But it didn't matter now. When I get back, he told himself, I'll throw it in her face before she can say anything about my crashing the plane. I'll accuse her of being a slut, which is what she is, right? And she'll cower from my rage and be afraid. Or, at least, begin showing some respect, which she's never really done. Well, she will now, and she damn well better show me some respect now.

And then he wondered, maybe she isn't such a slut, maybe she's only afraid I'll let her down. Maybe she just needs a man, a real man she can look up to? Isn't that what they always say? That a woman needs a *real* man, someone who is stronger than her.

Okay, but maybe *this* is what I've needed all my life, a real challenge? A challenge that needs to be met and overcome, conquered. Well, he thought, this desert is challenge enough for any man.

He watched the small round cone-shaped mountain as he came closer to it. It wasn't as small as he'd thought. It's only a hill, he thought, but he decided he'd continue to think of it as a mountain. It was nearly conical and covered with black jagged rocks, but he rejected the idea it might be volcanic. Of course, it isn't a volcano, he thought. He wondered what sort of freak of nature had put it there, and then decided he should climb it. He hoped climbing it would stop him from thinking about the ache in his gut, and besides, he might be able to see something from up there.

It was three in the afternoon when he finally reached his mountain. The sun had passed overhead and was on the other side of the hill so that he was standing in its shadow. He sat down in the shade and looked up, studying it while he rested. He'd been certain there wasn't any water in the plane, but now he berated himself for not searching for it anyway. It really doesn't seem tall enough to be classified as a mountain, he thought, but I will think of it that way anyway. For some reason, he thought of the Tower of Babel.

He sat in the shade and after a while, a breeze came up. A breeze to cool my sweat, he thought, if I had any left. He laughed. But it was smart to be sitting here now, he thought. A little bit of heaven out in the desert. He lay back against a rock and closed his eyes, and before long he was asleep. He dreamed of a black alley cat chasing a field mouse in an empty parking lot.

It was his stomach and his burning throat that woke him. It was late in the afternoon, with maybe only an hour or so of daylight left. He stood up, deciding that it would be best to climb the mountain now, to see if he could see the highway.

He put his jacket back on and began to climb. The base of the little mountain was very rocky, with large boulders here and there among the smaller ones. At first, it didn't seem too steep, and he moved quickly, hurrying because he didn't want to climb back down in the dark. But he became very tired before he was even halfway up. There were fewer rocks now, but the sand was loose, making the climb more difficult. He slipped and nearly fell several times, grabbing out with his hands and tearing his fingers. He wondered if anyone had ever climbed this mountain. Probably not, he decided. Probably nobody knew it existed. But he would tell them about it.

The going got steeper, and he had to use his hands as well as his feet to make any gain. His hands were torn and sore, but he told himself it was only part of the ordeal.

When he was almost in reach of the top he slipped and slid back down about ten or twelve feet, ripping the knees of his pants and skinning his knees. Now his knees burned as much as his fingers. But he edged his way around to the west until he reached the sunlit side and found a small ledge to rest on. He looked around. There was the highway, all right. Just a mile or less away. A truck happened to be passing just at that moment, looking like a toy in the distance. Victor waved his arms and tried to yell but his voice croaked. The sun was dropping behind the mountains, but Victor decided to rest a little before climbing down. Once he got to the highway, he could catch a ride into the nearest town and use the payphone. Tell them how he walked out of the desert. He smiled, closing his eyes.

When he heard the helicopter, he opened his eyes and stood up quickly, waving his arms, trying to find it in the darkening sky. Then he heard the rattlesnake behind him. Panicking, he tripped and fell, rolling and tumbling almost halfway down the hill. When he stopped, he saw that his right leg was twisted oddly. He knew it was broken but searched in vain for a snake bite.

The helicopter landed at the bottom of Victor's Hill, as it came to be known, and Sam and the pilot climbed up and somehow managed to carry him down. His wife, Angie, was with them. She was very angry with Victor and wasted no time before berating him for stopping to climb a silly little hill when the damn highway was right over there.

#2

The willowed lousy horse's blare
sets its hollow bread stakes there
While yonder aching tire-cubs rend
searching honey grass watchers mend
As silly sea-gory twerpers romp
sightless oblong crawlers flip
and flop

WARRIOR'S LAMENT

At least the sun shines
At least the moon glows
And the flowers rising
And the trees blooming
And all the things that grow
White moonbeams on waters gleam
Sunlight flashes in the stream
A thousand horses stand upstream
Could I really dream this dream?
Snakes across the river crawl
Bugs and things await my fall
Ten thousand horses still well upstream
Would that it only be a dream
Across the river a petal falls
Lands among all that crawls
While on the tree a fresh bud blooms
Up the river I sense my doom
And now the horses stand so near
I taste the quiet taste of fear
Among my men a solemn grows
Now there is nothing left to know
And as all around me brave men fall
I see a sparrow rise
Catch the wind

And fall

Jesus Ramirez

Jesus Ramirez was a big man with brown skin and strong coarse hands. His was a strong face, but the skin was soft and tender, and a fine black stubble would grow around his chin and cheeks whenever he didn't shave for a few days. Jesus looked at his hands. The little black hairs curled tightly against his brown skin and the fingernails were broken and curled underneath.

He sat on the flat hard bed inside his cell, and he felt the cold rising inside his gut. The cell was too small, cold and bare, and held no life except his own. There were no windows to see the sky or to let a breeze blow in, just the walls and bars and the hum of the fans blowing in the white corridor outside the cell.

"Hey Ramirez," Sammy called from the adjoining cell.

"Yes."

"It's almost time."

"I know."

"Are you afraid?"

"I don't know."

"I am," said Sammy. "I'm afraid already. I wouldn't blame you for being afraid."

"I don't know if I am."

There was a silence in Sammy's cell for a long time, then finally Sammy spoke very quietly.

"Have you confessed?"

"Yes," he lied.

"That's good, then. I have also confessed, although I don't think it will do me any good. But I will pray for you, Ramirez."

"Why?" asked Jesus Ramirez.

"Because I believe you are a good man, of course."

"Then I will pray for you as well," said Jesus Ramirez, thinking to himself: Yes, I will pray. We pray for one another, hoping God will understand our needs and our sins.

After a while, Jesus Ramirez rolled over onto his stomach in the hard narrow bed. His feet were hurting him, and he could not remember his feet ever hurting him before his trial began, many months before. The pain had slowly increased over time, and they were aching very hard now.

To take his mind off his feet he began to think of things from his youth. His mother had been a beautiful woman with dark brown eyes and skin that was almost white, and her long soft hair had been as black as his own. She had been so good to him, as she was to his brothers, and to his father. He remembered the violent red sunsets and the sugar cake cookies his mother had given to them with their tea in the evenings under the stars in the desert of Mexico. He thought of the guitar his mother played as his father and brothers sang happy songs, and it seemed to him it had always been like that when he was a boy.

But she had died when he was only ten years old, and everything changed after she was gone.

He had been sad and lost and a little angry, but the worst was to come, for his two brothers were even angrier and changed in the way they treated their little brother, while his father was suddenly not his father anymore, for all his love was gone out of him. So, the little anger that he felt at first when his mother was taken away had grown and risen inside, becoming cold and vicious anger towards everyone, so that he began fighting with other boys at school, and finally made enemies of his father and his brothers when they eventually tried to help him. Eventually, that had passed and left him a man, and he had gone out to face the rest of the world, which to him was a new world, the world called America, Los

Unidos. And there had been many women along the way. Too many, and he wondered now if he had been too hungry for love.

"Ramirez!" The guard was standing in the hallway.

"Yes."

"Do you want the priest?"

Jesus Ramirez thought about it. He had not been to the church but once since his mother died, and that had been after his great sin. He had confessed not to a priest but instead to his namesake hanging on a wall, so perhaps it wouldn't hurt to confess now.

"Yes," he said. "Thank you."

The priest came and he was an old man, older than Jesus Ramirez would ever be. He was almost bald but what hair he had was snow white and his head looked pink and bright in the light when he stood in the corridor waiting while the guard opened the cell.

He gave the sign of the cross when he stepped inside, saying a soft prayer before sitting next to Jesus Ramirez on the small hard bed.

"Hello, Father," Jesus Ramirez said.

The priest only nodded, taking out his beads.

"I won't need those," said Jesus Ramirez.

"No? What do you need, my son?"

"I do not know, Father."

"Are you afraid of death?"

"I think I can feel the fear coming, Father."

"We all must die, my son."

"I'm not afraid of death, Father. The chair itself is what I fear."

"Everyone must die in the ordinary course of life. But you are being punished."

"I'm not sure anymore. I no longer feel dirty."

"We all must face our sins. You have sinned greatly by taking the lives of others, and it is the law of this land that spells out your punishment. Perhaps it is a fair and equal and just law, and perhaps it is not. But the word of God says you can be forgiven for your sins, and that is a good law. Will you confess your sins and beg God's forgiveness?"

"I only felt dirty before I killed the two evil ones," said Jesus Ramirez, his eyes glowing with the redness of deep hatred.

The priest had to swallow hard, watching the prisoner's eyes.

"Why did you feel you had to kill them?"

"They were too dirty, Father. They made me dirty. They made me do evil things. They were dirty, like wild dogs, both of them."

"Why didn't you just leave them?"

"Because...I don't know. There were too many women before them. I loved so many of them, and some of them tried to love me. But those two didn't want my love."

"Nor to give it?"

"Nor to give. They wanted only my soul."

The priest looked sadly at the palm of his hands.

"You should be at peace with your soul. At peace with the Lord Jesus Christ."

"I think I am, Father."

"You should ask for His forgiveness."

"They were worse than whores.

"They were living beings."

"No, they were dead. Dead before I killed them."

THE PRIEST PRAYED WITH Jesus Ramirez before he left the cell, leaving Jesus Ramirez alone once more. He lay back down on his stomach on the flat hard bed with his eyes open and stared into the dark corner of his cell, listening to the water dripping into the little sink next to his bed. His eyes stung a little now, and he could smell the stink of the toilet in the other corner. His feet didn't hurt so much now, but he could feel what must be the fear building up from his stomach into a tight knot in his chest. Rolling over onto his side, he wondered how it would be. Now the things he remembered seemed so long ago, and he saw them in snatches, like in a photo album. The first coldness of the air in autumn along lonely railroad tracks through the desert. The hot sun of summer where bulls scratched and snorted in the dust, and the warm blue of the Pacific Ocean when he had seen it for the first time. He remembered many long happy drunks and how it was to take the first drink, knowing many more would follow. He remembered the lovemaking and the sweetness and beauty of a certain dark young girls and their flower scents in the spring. He remembered his first time in a big city, looking for work and his trip to Argentina on a freighter and the smell of the Panama Canal at night.

It had been a full life, he thought. Even those two evil women had made his life somehow fuller, he thought now. He wished he had been able to understand them, even if he would have still had to kill them. Everyone had their own gamble with life, everyone had to play the cards they were dealt, but it did not seem to him now that he had lost. He thought that some people died being very tired of life and that those two had been tired, and he had only helped them.

"Hey, Ramirez," Sammy called.

"Yes."

"It's too damned quiet! Are they coming soon? I don't think I can take it being so damned quiet!"

"It's always quiet before death."

"It's making me nervous. I'm sorry to bother you."

"Why are you sorry? It's going to be okay."

"It makes me think of the war. It was always too quiet, somehow."

"Don't listen to the quiet," said Jesus Ramirez.

"I can hear them now. They are coming for you now," said Sammy with a sigh.

Jesus Ramirez listened.

Yes, they were coming now. When they reached his cell, he stood up for them. The priest was with them. Jesus waited until they opened the cell door and then stepped out and walked down the corridor with them. His shoulders seemed to lift and straighten as he walked by Sammy's cell.

Sometimes more

If nothing less
How far we reach, for something less
"Awake, awake", the Red Witch cried
"We're off, we're off, we musn't miss the tide!"
So, with morning's glory blazing sun behind us, we set sail
for deep blue waters to divide.
For lands unseen,
people who have never been,
a whole new world,
'neath stars never seen
"Where o' where, can this place be?
No one's ever shown it on a map to me.
Is it real, or is it me?
Is this the place where I am to be?
Yes, but...
Time settles in and rides along,
Colors take no and make them say yes
Trees and leaves become one
When all shades of dark and light combine
And yes and no
intertwine
And the songs we've sung
become things we've done
What is real, if nothing's not?

Yet sometimes more, if nothing less
How far we'll reach
For sometimes less.

COLD NIGHT
ON PALOMAR MOUNTAIN

Staring into the fire
I felt the hard rocks beneath me
Staring into the fire
I felt the cold wind behind me
Staring into the fire
I heard the frogs sing below me
Staring into the fire
I felt her love all around me
What could be lacking
Staring into the fire?

ESPECIALLY

Sunset, sunset
Another day's energy sent
As life flows
Shri flows
Like two rivers
They merge
Firefly lady, we loved you

Taking its sweet time

Blank paper
staring me in the face
Demanding a story
Hopefully
some words of grace
But I
seeking something elusive
To call *the truth*
See no chance
of any words
Taking place

ONCE UPON A TIME
ON A GRASSY KNOLL

"Hi," she said.

"Hello," he answers without looking at her.

"Are you meditating? I don't mean to disturb you."

"No, you're not disturbing anything."

"I couldn't help noticing you sitting here. You've been so still."

He doesn't respond and the silence seems to stretch.

"So, mind if I join you?" she asks, trying to sound anything but nervous.

"No, not at all."

She sits, looking around at the trees and shrubs. "It's such a lovely day!" she says.

"Oh yes."

"Oh, look at that pretty blue bird," she says, pointing, her eyes lighting up.

"I wonder what it is? Is it a bluebird or a jay? I don't know my birds at all, do you?"

He looks but doesn't answer.

"Oh good, you're smiling now. I was afraid you never would. You've got a nice smile." She has been speaking too quickly, she realizes and looks away from him in embarrassment.

"Thank you," he says, finally.

"Shit," she says.

"What's wrong?"

"Oh, nothing. I was being too weird, that's all. I'm always being too weird."

He thinks about this, and after a moment says, "I don't believe you were being too weird, not in the least. Anyway, everyone's a bit weird sometimes, aren't they?"

"Well, there. You're smiling again." She is looking into his eyes but looks away again after another long moment of silence.

The silence continues. He must be listening to the wind, she thinks madly. Her thoughts are racing. Should she leave, should she stay, who is this guy? What is he thinking? He probably thinks I want to jump him. Oh, shit! But he is so cute!

Meanwhile, the sun is baking their backs as they sit silently on the grassy hill.

"I should be going," she says finally.

"No, please. You should stay. We can talk if you want. It's nice here, isn't it?"

"Oh yes, it's very nice." She has drawn her knees up to her chest and is studying her toes in the grass.

"So, were you meditating? You were sitting so still for such a long time, and with your legs crossed like that you looked like a Yogi."

"No. I was only resting."

"Well, you sure looked like a Yogi, sitting that way."

"It's very comfortable."

"Yeah. Most guys can't sit that way though. Not for very long. They get all squirmy and stuff."

"I'm limber enough, I suppose."

"I took some yoga classes once."

"Did you like them?"

"Yeah." She squints at the sun, still very warm, which is shining in their faces now.

"I'm going to get back into it."

"Good."

He has closed his eyes again, is facing the sunlight.

"Listen. Do you hear?"

She looks at him, and smiling, closes her eyes.

"I can hear the wind," she says. She is listening very hard, but there is only the wind in the trees and some distant traffic noise.

"Well, just listen."

"My heart," she answers after a while.

She has remembered to relax, thinking of the yoga lessons she once took.

"Listen," he repeats softly.

She is listening. A jet is flying high overhead, approaching the nearby airfield. And she hears birds chirping and singing, children playing nearby, but she says nothing of these things. She is listening very carefully, she thinks.

"I don't hear anything!" she says finally.

"Yes, that's because it's so damned quiet, isn't it?" he says finally, and with that, they both start laughing hysterically, rolling in the grass.

KOTO, GHIGLIA

See the quiet
rice fields
Sense the timeless toil
and the Matador
So tall and thin
Stalking his kill
An evening's music
Is filled with years

HELLO!

A guiding light
burst
Upon my new year
fading dreams cast
New reflections
From all the mirrors
of my mind

A LONELY NIGHT OUT

Late in the night, he awoke. He stared at his dark ceiling for a while, then slowly and painfully turned on his side to see the clock on the nightstand next to his bed. It was two o'clock in the morning and old man Carson sighed.

After he had laid there for another half an hour he reached over and turned on the lamp next to the clock. Its bulb flickered once and he was in darkness again. Cursing softly, he groped for his slippers in the dark. He knew his search for sleep was over for this night.

He stepped into the short hallway and turned on the overhead light, then went back into his bedroom to find his robe in the closet. "Now," he said aloud to himself, "I'll go see about something to eat."

He fixed himself a ham sandwich on wheat bread with mustard and a single leaf of green lettuce and a dill pickle on the side. And a glass of water from the sink faucet.

As he ate Carson read a story in an adventure magazine, which told about a young girl living alone in the countryside on an old farm. Two men came in the night and forced her to let them hide there. Another man drove off the road the next day and stopped to ask for directions, but the men jumped him and tied him up, planning on stealing his car. Then the men began to molest the girl and the stranger got loose from his ropes and saved her. He had to kill the two bandits. The girl cried and threw her arms around the stranger. The stranger told the girl he had to leave before the police came, that he had to be somewhere else, and the girl kissed him then, sadly. The man drove off on the dusty farm road. Carson thought it was a very sad story.

After he had finished his meal and the story, he lit his pipe and sat still at the kitchen table, staring at the wallpaper and listening to the water dripping in his kitchen sink. He wondered why he was unable to sleep well anymore. Perhaps it was the weather, or he was truly getting old. Now Carson smiled at himself. It was summer again, and in his younger days, when Ann was still alive, they would spend their summer nights with their friends, or out on the pier fishing, or enjoying a movie in town. Ann had loved to go see a movie. She had always said that he resembled the actor Clark Gable. Even without the mustache, she would say.

"No," he always answered her, "I think I look more like Powell."

But it was true in that Carson had large ears and eyes that sometimes twinkled, even now. And his nose and smile were something like the film star, or at least Ann thought so. But Gable and his wife were dead and Carson lived on with his nearly white hair and bad knees.

Carson sighed aloud. His pipe had gone out. He wasn't sure why he bothered with it anymore, but he lit another match and held it over the bowl of the pipe until it was well lit. Maybe it is just these old habits that keep me awake, he thought.

He rose from the table and went out of the kitchen, turning the light off. He sat in the small living room in the darkness. Tomorrow, he said to himself, I will have to go down to Henry's and get some light bulbs. Or else he would have no light to read by in his bed. How could he fall asleep without reading in bed? And he needed some coffee, there was little left, only enough for another pot, which he would make at dawn. And maybe some sweet rolls too. Ann had always liked them at breakfast. Carson prided himself that he still had all of his teeth, and he normally avoided sweets of any kind. But the rolls suddenly sounded wonderful.

Carson liked to go down to Henry's store. The little neighborhood market was only a few blocks away and his knees didn't complain too much. Henry was a fat old Mexican who cussed in Spanish at his white son-in-law and grandkids who helped out in the store sometimes, even though Carson was pretty sure none of them spoke Spanish. Henry's face would split into a huge yellow smile whenever Carson came through the door. He would help Carson find what he needed and then would say, "Carson, my friend. When will you grow wise and move away from this little slum town?" he said, grinning as always.

"I like it here, it's a fine little town."

"I would move if I were you. These punks now, in this part of town, they are getting much too wild nowadays. Someday one of them will roll you down in the gutter and take your wallet."

"They won't find much," Carson would say, and smile. He had lived in his house too long to want to move away and live surrounded by strangers. And there was the memory of Ann.

Carson liked Henry but Henry did not play chess, only poker, checkers, or dice games. He tried a few times but always threw up his hands in frustration, cursing in Spanish good-naturedly. So, they often played a few games of checkers in the backroom instead. It passed the day. Carson did miss playing chess with Ann, who had nearly always won.

Carson sat now in the dark of his living room and smoked his pipe, thinking of these things. It was still a few hours before dawn, and he looked out his front window and saw how the summer morning breeze was moving the leaves on the trees. He decided to go outside and walk a little. He would go to Henry's later in the morning, and he looked forward to it.

He dressed and went out. The morning breeze felt cool on his face, but there were only a few stars in the sky. The smog and the haze and the city lights hid them. There were never any stars anymore, he thought. It didn't matter though, because he didn't trust the stars anymore. They lied. They were so far away that they were probably dead really, and the light from them wasn't real. They might all be dead, he thought, but I will die long before their light fades.

He enjoyed the walk. He enjoyed the trees and the rustling of their leaves in the breeze. The trees didn't lie. Neither did the wind. And he enjoyed the front yards and their family clutter. Nearly every house showed signs of children. It's strange, he thought, what you can see when you look.

He finished his walk by standing on his front lawn under the old oak tree. He put his hand out, touching the bark to lean on it, and stood that way for a little while. Then he heard the girl's voice from behind him and he froze.

"But is it safe down here?" Her voice came from under his old wooden porch.

"Yeah, baby. Only a deaf old man lives here."

"I trust you so much," said the girl.

"This is a very safe place," said the boy's voice.

Carson stood very still, trying not to hear the sounds of the lovemaking, but he smiled and thought about Ann and their first time together, in New Orleans so long ago.

When they had finished and crawled out from under his porch, Carson tried to stay out of sight behind the old oak's trunk. The girl was dusting herself off dreamily, but the boy saw him. He nudged the girl and she looked at Carson and then ran away. The morning was just beginning to light the sky in the east. The boy strode angrily toward Carson and glared at him, his fists bunched tightly.

"Lonely night out or something Mister? Or do you just like sneaking around for kicks or something?"

"No," Carson said. "This is my house and I couldn't sleep." And then he went inside and got back into his bed.

#3

Lately spins the upper down
moonlight flickers
and waves go round
and round
(he saw rainbows)
when the new
begins in old
And in earnest
songs are told
(he heard music)
And as the how
became the didn't
Somewhere in difference
there was the same
(he felt their pain)

YOU

Magic Lady
All aglow
When now I see you
(heart sits bare)
And when now I don't
(nothing matters anywhere)
Yet such a little
Touch of glow
Passed between our fingers so
That set my heart
Set it right
Made me want to dance all night
So, when now I see you
(heart's on fire)
And when now I don't
(can only wonder if you care?)
I know my freedom's won
When my hear says so
And when I see you
(heart's on fire)
And when I don't
(can't sink this heart, can't sink it no)
I think I love you
my heart says so

#4

Can the mellow
Halt the hard
Can the meadow
Be your yard
Can the bad
Be your good
Can the senseless
Be understood
Can the guilty
Be absolved
Can the hopeless
Get involved
Can a train
Roll uphill
Can that silence
Be an air raid drill
Can the false
Be so true
As to ever
Get through to you

#5

Here the prevailing winds
Blow down through the lush green valley
Now hard, now soft
I hear them
I can feel them
"what's that song again?"
Warm wet green light fills my morning
And out there
Jungle leaves stir
"I've got it, I've got it sir!"
Blown down, it's all blown down
I'll crush, I'll crush, I'll hug them all
Then I'll run and hug the ground
"What's that song again?"
Here the prevailing winds
Blow down through the lush green valley
Bringing rain
That fills the holes
Now hard, now soft
"This is the end, this is...."
My only friend

Song of the Ortega

Sometimes more
if nothing less
how far we reach
for something less
"Awake, awake," the young ones cried,
"We're off, we're off! We musn't miss the tide!"
So with mornings glory blazing sky behind us
we set our sails
deep blue waters to divide.
For lands unseen
people that have never been
a whole new world
'neath stars never seen.
Where, oh where, can this be seen?
Has anyone ever shown it
On a map to me?
Is it real, or just a dream?
Is this the place where I am to be?
And I say yes...but then...
time will move to remind
life is free...here and gone
colour's take no
and turn them yes
and leaves and trees are seen as one

where first and last
intertwine
all shades of dark and light
combine
When songs we've sung
become things we've done...
how far we reach
for sometimes less.

Night Lights

Lakes of wet green grass
where
Tall trees stand so still
In the cool sea air
A lone gull flies
And I can only sit
and stare.
How clear, how bright
This cold star night
How still and calm
This ocean's balm.
Then...
With the lone gull's cry
small waves begin to sigh
a cool sea breeze shivers
in my ear
and stirs the leaves
in those tall trees.
And while I watch and listen
So carefully
I only manage to barely see
one bright star
Shut its eye
And wink at me!

THIS IS YOUR SONG

Hey Gaili
It's been a long, long time
There's never been another
In all the misty
Mountain time
Hey Gaili
all those years ago
you came back out west
and walked into my kitchen
making all the waiters say
"ain't she so bitchin'!"
oh, I swelled up
filled with pride
knowing deep down
deep inside
that you'd only come
To say goodbye again
Hey Gaili
In all the misty
Mountain time
You're not forgotten
I'll miss you forever
was it really
Only a few happy days

we ever spent together?
Hey Gaili
I still have your letters
can't read them anymore.
Hey Gaili
you made the mold
set the bar so high
none could follow,
it never got old.
So, I can try
But won't forget
Even if I cry
Hey Gaili,
Ride safe and far,
It's always hard
To say goodbye.

The Spaceman

It was another typical southern California winter morning, sunny and clear, with only high wispy white clouds streaming eastward across the sky, indicating the winds were blowing hard at that altitude. Tom stood in the small yard of the little cottage he rented, situated behind the much larger home of his landlady, Mrs. Hamm. Here on the hill above the beach town below, there was no wind blowing at all, and Tom's first thought that morning was that the waves would be pretty good. Something in the air itself, he thought, or the promising early warmth of the winter sun on his back, some memory of other mornings, told him the waves would be good. He sighed quietly and going out the back gate into the alley, started walking down the long hill into the village below. Because of the crowds, he never went surfing on Sundays anymore.

It was a fair walk down into town, but the sun was warm on his back, and the view of the orderly streets below laid out east to west and north to south, with the wide silver-blue ocean, dotted with small offshore islands, leading to the horizon. He could see what was probably a good four-foot swell hitting this part of the coast below, but even from this distance, he could see how the water was scattered with little black dots near the pier, where the best waves were breaking. He wasn't going to let the crowding bother him, deciding to focus instead on enjoying his Sunday breakfast at the Village Café and reading his usual Sunday newspaper. Later he would get together with his girlfriend, Sandi, and they would find something to do together. Maybe another day in the City Park, throwing a frisbee with Steve and Sigrid, or an afternoon matinee movie downtown. He decided it would be a fine day either way, whatever they did. Since he worked nights during the week, he could always get some surfing in on a weekday morning. No biggie.

It was more crowded than usual at the restaurant, so after purchasing his paper from the newsstand next door, Tom found a seat on the long narrow counter near the large front window, rather than his usual booth in the back. He had half-expected this, so it didn't bother him too much. He didn't see anybody he knew in the crowd anyway, although many faces were familiar. The Townhouse was always crowded until well past noon on Sunday mornings, and Dottie, the waitress serving the counter, seemed barely able to give him a preoccupied-looking smile when she came to pour his coffee and take his order. He couldn't blame her, the place was busy serving every sort of person one could imagine, from young hippies to old codgers and the usual hung-over regulars. But coming here on Sunday mornings was his habit and had been for the last ten years or so. Well, nearly so. There was his trip to Hawaii two years back. That had lasted a few months, but he didn't think he'd ever go back. It was better to spend his time and money traveling south to the uncrowded surfing spots in southern Mexico and Central America. Maybe, he thought, he'd one day try going over to Ireland. Rumors of excellent waves breaking on nearly empty reefs were just beginning to spread. So what if the water was cold?

His mind was wandering, he realized. He began to read his newspaper, reading the comic pages first, and enjoyed his breakfast when it came. Once he'd finished eating, he rolled the paper up and was paying his bill at the counter when he noticed a disturbance outside, and loud voices coming in the doorway.

"That guy's crazy, man!"

"Nah, he's just trippin'."

"Weirdo."

"Wow, he's freaking me out!"

Tom tried to ignore all of this as he pushed through the crowd in front of the door, but then he saw even more people gathering in a circle around an odd-looking little man in the middle of the street. He wore baggy brown pants, a long-sleeved green shirt with rolled-up sleeves, and a wide-brimmed straw hat like the ones that lifeguards wore on duty. He had no shoes, and his feet were nearly black with dirt. He looked altogether like the typical bum who lived along the sandy beaches just to the north. He was an older man, his white hair was sticking out in places from under the hat, and his eyes had a wild look. He was babbling something that Tom tried to ignore as he turned away, intending to walk home.

"You folks gotta believe me! I saw what I saw, I'm telling you! It's a warning, that's what. What else could it be? And this is where it stopped, man. I'm here, but I ain't from here, see. I'm only here cuz this is where it dumped me off."

"Where are you from, then?" someone asked.

"I don't know if I'll ever get back. It quit working after it brought me here, as far as it wanted to go, I guess." The old man was speaking more calmly now. He laughed. "Heh, I started out in nineteen and forty-six, heh."

"Started out?"

"Yeah, see. I ain't dumb, I saw the dates on car license plates, see? I ain't dumb. And those cars, golly, they sure are something nowadays." He was speaking evenly but his eyes and general expression were still very excited, staring from face to face as if he was searching for one that expressed belief.

"Prove it, old man. Where is this machine, show it to us."

Tom had stopped to listen, his curiosity aroused. A young girl stood next to him with her bicycle, watching the scene with a seemingly detached air that Tom knew was intended to be aloof, so typical of the young surfer girls in town. She looked vaguely familiar, tan, and pretty, and he decided he'd probably seen her out in the water surfing near the pier. She noticed him, her face breaking into a wide toothy smile.

"Hey, Tom!"

"Hi," he said, feeling foolish. What was her name?

"This guy's unreal," she said.

"Yeah, I guess." Yes! She was John Silverton's little sister! Becky, of course. All grown up now.

"Get away from me," someone was yelling, and Tom tried to look, but couldn't see the old man any longer, the crowd had closed in around him.

"What's going on, anyway?" he asked Becky. "I was having breakfast, and missed most of it."

"Oh, he was telling some story..." Her voice stopped when the man began yelling again, his voice coming from the middle of the crowd.

"I'm real! I'm real and I want a cop! Get off me!"

"Here's one now, old man! Here to save your ass,"

A patrol car was moving slowly up the street two blocks away, near the pier, and then the little old man was free from the crowd and running towards them waving his arms. Then someone screamed and there was the sound of screeching tires and a loud thump.

"Let's get out of here," Tom told Becky. The old man had been hit by a blue van turning too quickly out of the cross street half a block away. Tom felt sick, and the girl's tan face looked white. He pushed her bike for her as they walked up the hill.

"It was a time machine," she said. "He said he'd been brought here by a time machine."

"That's crazy."

"Yeah."

Tom felt he should say something, the girl seemed freaked out. "Well, that crowd wasn't helping things any."

"No," she agreed, looking up at him. She seemed very young.

"What else? Did he say anything else? Where's this time machine now, I wonder."

She stopped and turned to look back down the hill towards the crowded scene in front of the restaurant, where an ambulance was just arriving.

"I don't know, exactly," she said. "He was telling us that we need to slow things down, that we're wrecking our world, wrecking the environment. But I couldn't understand everything he said." She looked at Tom, her face nearly back to its normal color now. "He was talking about world ecology, you know? I think that's what he was saying, mostly. He didn't exactly say anything new, but..."

"Huh," said Tom. She looked so serious, but he couldn't think of anything to say.

Becky looked at him, shrugging her shoulders. She took her bike back, and holding the grips in her hands, she began to move the bars back and forth slowly, like shaking someone their head. "I'd better get home," she said.

"How's your brother, anyway?" Tom said, grinning. "Tell him I said, hey!"

Tom went home with his Sunday paper tucked up tightly under his arm, trying to stay calm. He was upset because reality had once again busted his perception of the world. There was always something bad happening anymore, he thought. Shootings, robberies, daylight rip-offs of people just innocently walking in the streets of the little town. He tried to ignore most of it, tried to focus on the good things instead, but he was tired of trying, and this morning's incident had been another grim reminder of reality. Crazy people were nothing new, of course. There was one old local, an artist who actually called himself '*The Spaceman*', and if you were nice enough to get on his good side, he would assign you an official boarding number to get you on the spaceship that would arrive at the end of the world, which would be very soon. Tom and another boy had helped the Spaceman con some fishermen in the harbor out of a few pounds of fresh mackerel one summer day, and each had been assigned an official number as a reward. Tom still remembered his number, you bet. You never knew, right?

Tom went inside his little house and turned on his stereo, turning it up just loud enough that he could hear it outside in his yard if he left his door open. He was tired of thinking and just wanted to sit in the sun and close his eyes for a while.

Tom put his little beach chair down facing the Sun and sat in it, his legs stretched out, the music relaxing him, the grass under his bare feet warm and alive. Leaning back in the chair, he closed his eyes, his eyelids red against the sun, and after a while, visions were swimming through his mind. A bottle of Apricot brandy, the Spaceman swigging from it as he drove his car towards the harbor, grinning at him in his rearview mirror. Becky's pale face, the blue van with its smoking tires, a policeman striding into the crowd with a determined look. A beautiful wave, empty and peeling perfectly, its face ruffled by the wind. He opened his eyes for a moment, lowering his gaze to see the familiar little yard his small house shared with Mrs. Hamm's house behind him, the high hedge hiding the alleyway, the tall avocado and lemon trees in the corners, and...what?

A small machine sat under the lemon tree. It looked like some sort of a double bicycle with four tall wheels and a black saddle. Tom stared at the contraption in disbelief. How had it gotten in the yard? It couldn't possibly belong to Mrs. Hamm. She was way too old, wasn't she? Once he'd awoken to find a dirty bearded bum sleeping in the yard, and he felt the same way now as then. Violated.

Tom stood up and moved with determined impetuousness, his face and eyes intense as he strode to the strange machine, his lips closed in a tight line, but his naturally curious mind was already easing his anger. What the heck was this thing?

It was obviously some sort of a machine, built out of what looked like plastic and some kind of dull metal, except for the seat, which looked just like real leather. It didn't have any handlebars, so it wasn't a bicycle, and besides that, the 'wheels' were nearly as tall as himself. There were however two levers and what looked like a large clock-faced dial between them. There was a long step on the side, reminding him of the running boards on a truck. Tom was torn by his sudden desire to climb into the thing and the idea that it would soon kill the lawn underneath if he didn't move it.

Tom slowly smiled as the idea finally dawned on him. It couldn't be, of course. No, it was only an idiotic coincidence. But what if it was? It was there, after all, and the desire to sit inside of it grew stronger as he gazed upon it. Well, the old man in the street this morning had certainly been real, that much was true.

Tom gently reached out to touch the machine, and something about the feel of it made up his mind, so he turned and quickly ran back into his house, where the suddenly overpowering loudness of his stereo wasn't even enough to give him pause. He grabbed his shoes, his toothbrush, his wetsuit, and his surfboard and put them behind the saddle of the machine. He ran back once more for a jacket and some long pants before he finally climbed up into the saddle, where he sat staring at the dial in front of him. Besides the dial, which only had one hand, there were just the two long levers on either side. No labels or instructions to tell him how to work anything.

"Eenie, meenie," Tom said, pulling hesitantly on the right-hand lever.

And suddenly everything went white, and the yard, the trees, his house, the hedge, everything vanished in that white flash, and he was alone and drifting through some sort of fog. Looking at the dial, he saw it rested now at what might be nine o'clock, but of course, he had no idea what the dial signified. Hours or days? Months or years? Tom pushed the lever back gently towards its original position, but nothing happened. He looked at the fog outside and saw that it ran underneath the machine as well. Was he flying? He couldn't detect any sensation of movement, but when he looked at the dial again he saw that it now rested at eleven o'clock. Shit! What had he gotten himself into?

Don't get excited, he told himself. At least it works. It's real, man, and you're on your way. No more of society's endless crap! I'll figure this thing out, find a good time to live in, and then come back to get Sandi and we'll live in paradise!

Tom pushed the left lever forward now, then watched in growing fear as the dial began spinning wildly counterclockwise. Nearing panic, he grabbed both levers, one in each hand, and began to push and pull on them in an effort to stop the dial from spinning. This was followed by the sudden sensation of the entire craft spinning and falling, and he had the feeling that he was going to be thrown out into the fog any second. Oh God, he thought, how do you stop this thing? He thought he must be screaming, and anticipating a hard landing, his feet searched for something to brace against. What was that, a pedal? Couldn't be, that would be too simple. He pushed against it with both feet, feeling mushy resistance. Then felt himself flying, cold air against his face, and a sudden, brutal impact.

Tom tried to open his eyes and found he was nearly blind, seeing only a vague blue fog. He tried to stand but fell on his stomach. The ground felt almost familiar under his palms, something like grass but not quite, and there was a strange, harsh odor in the air, like burnt toast. The harsh air felt both too dry and too cold. He lay still for a while longer, exploring his body with his mind. His knees and palms felt skinned and burned with pain, reminding him of his childhood. He hadn't had such a nasty spill in a long time. He felt a little dizzy and nauseous, and he didn't try to move again until his mind cleared enough to remember his surfboard and his other things. Crap! He should have tied his stuff down; he should have thought ahead. Then he thought he heard voices in the distance, far away, but voices, nonetheless.

Tom lifted his head slowly, not wanting to be sick, and the first thing he saw was the ocean. It was out there as always, looking silvery blue in the harsh hazy sunlight. The coastline looked familiar too, this must be the same part of it, but the familiar concrete fishing pier and the jetties and the man-made harbor were gone, replaced by some long black structure out near the horizon that stretched along the entire coast. Tom stared in utter amazement. He must be in the same place, but he'd gone forward in time, not back as he'd planned. He stood up and looked around. Yes, this was his hillside, but his little house and Mrs. Hamm's house and all the other houses were gone, as was any sort of pavement leading down into the village, where all the buildings were gone. Instead, everything was covered in what looked like a nice green lawn, but the grass looked too green to be real. It's like Astroturf, he thought. But there were lots of trees, lots of oak trees, and even some willows; it all looked like some sort of park, as far as he could see in any direction. No buildings. Except for that long black structure along the coast, which would surely block any swells from ever reaching the shore. And all along the shore was a wide band of what must be white sand, a perfect beach dividing the blue ocean and the green land. It looked like a cemetery. Tom looked everywhere, but there was no sign of the machine or any of his things. He was alone.

Tom stood on the hill, finding it difficult to catch his breath. The air had a strange smell that reminded him of dead things. He started down the hill, wanting to run but afraid he'd fall again, wanting to be in the ocean, to bathe himself in the salt water, but as he got closer to the shore, he saw that the tide was receding quickly, going further and further out, exposing a black dead bottom barely gleaming in the yellow haze of the sky.

He heard his name being called, and he fell. His lungs burned as he lay gasping for breath, finally seeing the truth. The grass, the trees, they were all fake. Oh God, he thought, wanting to scream, but his lungs hurt too much. What have they done to the world? And again, someone was yelling his name, closer now.

"Tom, Tom, wake up! Please, are you okay?" A hand slapped his face.

TOM OPENED HIS EYES to find Sandi and his landlady, Mrs. Hamm, standing over him. H was lying next to his little beach chair, which was overturned beside him in the grass. He looked up at his girlfriend, and feeling a great flood of joy, he pulled Sandi's face to his and kissed her on the mouth, at the same moment laughing into her lips with relief. She broke away with a giggle, and said, "Wow! That must have been some dream."

Steve and Sigrid were there with Sandi, and Steve helped Tom to his feet, Tom feeling slightly embarrassed by the whole thing. But he told them about his dream anyway, on their way to City Park, about the old man in the street that morning and his claims of a time machine, and even about the Spaceman, who Sandi said had died the year before. They threw the Frisbee in the grassy park, having a good time under the winter sun, and by the end of that fine day, Tom had nearly forgotten the whole thing.

#6

Where did all the rainbows go?
when I chased them
so long ago?
(Be fair, stand tall,
try to catch them all!)
don't look down
it's not safe you might fall
just might slip
and bust your hip!
Better not laugh
just might slip
bust your lip
Better not hide
just might slip
bust your pride
So, look for sun
bask in fun
(find someplace else to run)
But!
I found
along the way
an open heart
hears both sides
and unless you chase them

Rainbows never hide

#7

The three most powerful,
Sit, Small, and Off the Wall,
came together
for one and all
Sit said,
"I'd like to go
where others cannot go.
Wherever they can never go,
will be the only place I need to go!"
Small said,
"I'd like to grow
More than ten feet tall!
And grab what others
never reach at all!"
"Such dreams, such schemes,"
said Off the Wall,
"But remember friends,
Wherever you go,
wherever you rest,
it's best not to soil your jeans!"

FINDING NEVERLAND

Inside that ramshackle living room
filled with giant grown-ups
and their drunken laughter and fun,
the lampshade aviator
is making a gleeful run.
With his cardboard wings
His joy is to discover and populate
His secret world to elaborate.
And dreaming and scheming,
he knows he'll never, never
want to land.
It's not particularly funny
nor exactly sad,
watching his little noggin
beaming his private glad.
As he flies from the sink
bouncing off every window and wall
no parent will stop him!
nor the sad ghosts
in the hall
the lampshade aviator
will fly till he finds
his own Neverland.

The following story is excerpted from my novel, *Finding Rosie*:

FLORA (or Little Ed's Tale)

I leaned my chair up against the wall and gazed out the dirty tall narrow windows next to the doorway at the street outside. It was still early for that town, only 1000, and nothing was happening. The Clubs were still boarded up, with only a few vendors with their street stalls selling stuff. Drifty Glenn was sitting across the table from me, but we weren't talking much yet. It was too early, too quiet, and maybe it was just too much trouble to speak. Glenn was staring vacantly across the room, his mouth open. This expression was exactly why we called him 'Drifty', as he looked as if his mind had drifted off somewhere. Perhaps home to 'The World', which is what we called home. Right about now it would be 7 PM back in California, I figured, wondering what my wife might be doing at that very moment.

Shit! Gotta stay away from thinking about that shit! That's no good. You should know that by now. Stay away from that shit!

That's right, I thought. Okay.

"Let me have one of your smokes, Lil' Ed," said Glenn, grinning at me like a fool.

"Wipe that fool look off your face," I told him. He always used that expression whenever he begged a smoke, but it usually didn't bother me.

"Come on, man" he said.

"Take one then, Glenn."

He shook a cigarette out of the pack lying on the table between us and lit it with the lighter next to it. Then he put the lighter in his pants pocket, looking smug.

Slowly I pulled a smoke out of the pack before returning it safely into my shirt pocket.

"Okay, I'd like to use the lighter, Glenn."

"It's mine," he said.

"Yeah, so?"

"You know it is, right?"

"Yes. But I'd like to borrow it a minute."

"You borrowed it six months ago and never gave it back."

"That was when you said you were quitting, and didn't need it anymore." We went through this routine all the time.

"I don't smoke," he said, taking the lighter out of his pocket and holding it in front of me. "Not on base, anyways," he said, and took a drag on his cigarette before finally surrendering the lighter.

I lit my smoke and took a drink from my now warm San Miguel beer. "I wish you'd buy your own damn cigarettes though. You make more money than me anyway." I pocketed the lighter.

"Why won't you just buy another lighter?"

"All right. But you know I can only bring two packs out the gate at a time."

"You smoke too much anyway," Glenn said, exhaling a cloud of smoke. "Whatever happened to that fancy lighter you had, anyway?"

"You know what happened."

"Yeah, but I like hearing you tell the story."

"I hocked it. No big deal."

"Yeah. But where? And why?" He was grinning his famous *drifty grin* now.

"Yeah okay, I was broke, and maybe a little drunk. So? It woulda got stolen sooner or later anyway." I laughed.

"Yeah. But what did you do with the money? That's the part I like."

"Shut up," I said good-naturedly. I looked back out the window then and noticed a blue taxicab drawing up outside.

"Here comes your girlfriend," I said. "Here comes Flora."

"Oh great," said Glenn, putting his smoke out in the ashtray.

"You love her, and you know it," I told him. Now it was my turn to grin. Flora came in with her knitting stuff in her arms. She stopped at the table and didn't look at either of us. She looked terrible. A rough night, I thought. But then, there were no ships in port, none to speak of. Bad time for the hostess girls, bad time for the whole damn town. So it didn't make sense, her looking so tired and beat.

She dropped her knitting stuff and her purse on our table as she passed, and went back towards the head. Didn't say a word.

"What's up with her?" I asked Glenn. He looked solemn.

"Ah, she's just got some bug up her ass again," he said, trying to grin a little.

"Does she always look so depressed in the morning?"

"Well, she's a working girl."

"There aren't any ships in, Glenn."

He nodded, sipping his beer.

Flora came back after about 15 minutes to sit next to Glenn. She had washed her face, and I couldn't see any makeup. She had pulled her black hair back into a tight ponytail, making the brown skin of her forehead taut and almost shiny. The moment she sat she started knitting and didn't look at either one of us. I wondered if I should leave. It was still early to be out in town, but she was making me feel even less welcome than usual. Or something, anyway. Maybe I felt out of place.

"You want something to drink?" Glenn asked her.

Flora shrugged and didn't bother looking up from her knitting.

"Seven-Up?"

Her nod was nearly imperceptive.

"I'll get it," I said and rose quickly from my seat.

"Well," said Glenn, grinning at me.

Flora glanced up at me, but only for a second. Well, I was glad to get away from the table. Give them a minute alone, I thought. But I wouldn't leave the club. I didn't want to end up alone in town all morning, with nothing to do. Not in that town. And there was no way I'd go back on the base so early. So, I would have another beer and wait.

I made the girl at the bar chop some ice for Flora's Seven-Up. It took longer that way. The girl grumbled. Some of the Filipino people can be lazy when they want to be. I got another beer and paid two and a half Pesos for the beer and the soda. At six Pesos to a U.S. dollar, it was less than fifty cents. Not bad. When I first got there though, it had been four to one. Then a floating exchange rate was started, thanks to President Marcos. At times I've seen it go up to seven to one. At ten in the morning, in a dead quiet town in the humid heat, even one and a half Pesos for a San Miguel seemed too much. Nothing to be done about it. Sailors love to bitch and moan. I guess so.

When I went back to the table nothing had changed, Glenn still looked bored and drifty, and Flora concentrated on her knitting. I thought I could tell they had talked, though I don't know how I could tell.

Flora thanked me for the Seven-Up with a quick smile. She's not mad at the whole world at least, I thought. But it was Glenn who had paid for the drinks. I sat down and put his change on the table in front of him.

I sat looking through the window again for a while. Kong's restaurant, which I could barely see up the street, was open now. My stomach growled as soon as I noticed it. You need to get something to eat soon, I told myself. There were more people out walking around now. Girls and older women mostly. Going here and there, to the shops and beauty parlors. Even when the fleet was out and the town was dead quiet, some of the women would go to the beauty parlors anyway. It's the way they are, I thought, they need to look beautiful all the time. However, maybe they know about a ship coming in today. The hostesses always knew about any ships arriving before anybody else. If there was, it wouldn't be a big ship, like an aircraft carrier. I should know about it because of my job. I worked in Operations at the Naval Air Station Cubi Point. In the Crash/Fire crew, Port Duty Section. As did my pal *Drifty* Glenn Drake. Carriers had to send their aircraft in ahead, mostly, increasing our normal air traffic. So, I'd know about it, and there wasn't a carrier due in port for another few weeks. Carriers brought the most sailors and the most money into the town. Everybody knew that.

"I'll be back," Glenn announced as he rose slowly from his chair.

"Oh? Where ya going?"

"Toby's shoes. Gotta check on my boots."

"I don't feel like walking clear out there," I said.

"Good. You can stay here and keep Flora company."

Flora ignored us, knitting studiously.

"Okay," I sighed. "Hurry back."

"I won't be gone that long," he said. He turned and squeezed his long thin body between Flora's back and the table behind her. He started outside.

"I might be at Kong's," I said a little too quickly.

Glenn stopped at the door, looking back at us.

"Try and wait until I get back," he said. Then he went out into the brightness of the day. I looked at Flora. She was knitting, her fingers moving very quickly. She hadn't looked up to watch Glenn go. Christ, I thought. I wonder what he's done now? Or what she *thinks* he did?

I lit another cigarette and sipped my beer. This one was already getting warm. Man, what a day.

"What did Glenn tell you?" she asked me softly.

"About you?"

But she only shrugged.

"He never tells me anything."

"Oh well, if he didn't mention anything."

I sighed. She could be this way, and quite often was. It bugged me because I knew she was a groovy person when she was being herself.

When she wanted to be. I wanted to see her smiling, which I realized I hadn't seen in a while. See her happy, like the Flora I'd gotten used to. It would make this day better, I thought. She would go to lunch with us.

"Glenn never tells me anything," I said.

"Bullshit."

"No, really. Not about you and him, he doesn't."

"Bullshit," she said again. She missed a stitch then, and her mouth turned down in consternation.

"He doesn't talk about you. Sometimes, he might say, 'Oh we had a fight,' or something. But that's all."

She shrugged "He never tells me anything. I don't care."

"Well, I care," I told her.

"Why?"

"I just do. I care about my friends."

"So, you care about him. But I don't anymore."

"Oh, c'mon, we're friends too," I told her. "Tell me!"

Flora looked at me. For a moment she looked like her old happy self, as she grinned, looking into my eyes across the little table. She was pretty when she smiled. Then it was gone and she was staring down at her knitting again. She shrugged.

"Am I your friend, Flora?"

"Okay. Yes. We are friends."

"So, tell me."

"Maybe Glenn, maybe he doesn't want you to know? Maybe he'll get mad."

"But you said you don't care anymore."

"I don't care about him," she said. "Maybe I don't like him anymore. But I care about his baby."

I LEFT THE BAR AND crossed the Jeepney crowded street to order some fried rice for lunch at Kong's Restaurant. Kong's was airy and light and cool inside, and it was crowded as usual with town girls. They sat in little groups scattered around the dining room at the square tables gossiping in *Tagalog*. I imagined they were either telling one another about their current boyfriend, if they were lucky enough to have one, or maybe about last night's customer. Only that day, I knew there had been few if any customers the night before. There are over one thousand nightclubs and bars in the town of Olongapo City, and a dozen or more women, called *hostesses*, worked in each of them. That's a good estimate anyway because some of the clubs I know of have up to forty girls on their roster. Oh, it's a sailor's paradise all right. It's well known by sailors of every nation. It's the Sin City of the Orient. Sooner or later every sailor and Marine spends part of his life and lots of his money here. Something he'll never forget.

Then there are the guys like me who get stationed ashore here. *Station sailors*, the townies call us. Glenn and I had been here 10 months now, with eight more to go. But Flora had been here forever. This was her world. It was hard to remember that fact sometimes.

I ordered a Coke with my fried rice. You didn't drink milk in town. *Ever.* Unless it was canned sweet milk with coffee. And you drank the water only if you had to. You either drank beer or sodas, or sometimes cherry brandy or vodka or whiskey. Or even rum. Some of the places had pretty good rum. Rum is a tropical drink, isn't it? Maybe you drank whiskey once in a while, when somebody, somehow, got it out the gate, off the base. Anyway, the cokes always tasted flat here. It was said they made them that way, and you'd get used to it. Well, as long as they were cold.

The fried rice in Kong's was usually very good. Sometimes it was great. A friend of mine, called Buzzy, who is a lifer E6, but a very cool guy, claims he got food poisoning at Kong's once. Said he would never eat there again. He told Glenn and me we were nuts to eat there, and told us that all the time. But we would keep eating there until we got poisoned too. We were stubborn that way. I guess you had to be that way, living there.

But that day the fried rice didn't jazz me. I wanted Glenn to come back from his errand with his boots. I wanted to ask him what he was going to do about Flora. To find out how he felt about the situation.

Flora was cool and funny and friendly. There was something else too. She was lovable, I guess. I liked her for those things, even though I knew she was a *working girl*. She wasn't what I would call a whore. Or even a prostitute. She was what we called a working girl, in a town where there weren't many options for young women. Flora sold her time and companionship to lonely sailors who had been at sea fighting in a war nobody back home cared about. If she actually slept with some of them from time to time, I didn't really know or care. Even if she did, it didn't make her a whore. Not in my opinion. Mostly the hostess girls only danced and laughed with the men while they got drunk in town on Liberty.

But sometimes I wondered about my friends. Maybe they were using these girls. A free lay. I didn't think it was true of Glenn and Flora, not really. If you are stationed here long enough and you don't resist it, you will end up with a free lay of your own, a *girlfriend*. To the girls, a *station sailor boyfriend* was a kind of status symbol. Or at least it seemed that way to us. The girls all knew that the real money was only to be made when the ships were in port for Liberty. The sailors and Marines on the ships were very horny, wanted to party, and had plenty of cash. And the working girls in town, the Hostesses, were ready to entertain them. And those of us who had been there a while, we knew to stay out of their way. Personally, I lived for the quiet times in town, and I knew Glenn did too.

Of course, after months or years, a girl working in that town can get pretty bitter. She might decide she hasn't a chance of catching a good husband and stop playing the game. No station sailor boyfriend, no real men friends among the Americans, only the sad, dark nights when the ships were in and the money was flowing.

Glenn and I, and most of our buddies, not only respected the situation but did our best not to push it, to not take advantage, while at the same time knowing there were many in town willing and able to take advantage of us. At any time.

Sometimes a guy finds a special girl, marries her, and takes her home, back to *the world*. Sure, it happens. But the girls don't seem to trust it happening to them. And a girl has to work, boyfriend or not, to survive.

Glenn finally came in, just as I finished my rice.

"I thought you were going to wait for me."

"What about your boots?" I asked, feeling I had to say something.

"They're not ready."

"Figures."

"Toby said maybe by Monday. I told him they'd better be, or no deal."

"Attaboy," I said.

"Shit."

I lit a cigarette, stalling. I wanted to ask him the obvious question but wasn't sure how to phrase it. He was the best friend I had here. In the Navy. In the PI. We'd done the whole deal together, practically since boot camp. And he was from my hometown too, although we hadn't known each other back home. Different high schools. But I liked Flora. I guess I was afraid to ask. I guess if Glenn hadn't been 3 years younger than me, I wouldn't have said a word. Not right then anyway. But I did.

"Flora told me the news," I said, finally.

Glenn looked at me, staring. But I was looking right back at him, watching his eyes.

He grinned. "Shit," he said and looked away.

"Well?"

"I don't know," he said, looking back at me. "I figured this would happen, sooner or later. Dumb broad."

"Dumb broad? Whaddya mean? You don't think she's pregnant on purpose, do you?"

"I don't know what I think."

"The pill?"

"Maybe she forgot to take it. On purpose or not, I don't know."

"It turns out the same either way," I said.

"Yeah. Lemmee bum another smoke, man."

I handed the pack to him. "What's she going to do?"

"Didn't she tell you?"

"No, and I didn't ask."

"She's being righteous. She's going back home, back to her mother up in the province."

"Oh. And you? What does she want you to do?"

"Nothing. Says she's going to keep the kid to 'remember me' by."

"Oh man," I said, and I could see it on his face. He didn't have to say it, but he said the words anyway.

"It's my kid," he said quietly. "Here in the PI forever. A little *joe* who will look like me. Imagine that."

"How far along is she?" I asked, a bit desperate for something to say.

"Almost two months."

"Jesus."

"Far out, ain't it, man?" Glenn tried making his usual weird grin but was failing.

"And she just now told you? This morning?"

"That's right. I knew something was up, something bugging her, but..."

"She doesn't look it," I said. And felt stupid for saying it.

"That's a *Jo-anna* for you," he said, with the sick-looking grin again.

I nodded.

"She had to tell me, though," he said with a quick grin. "I mean, I see her naked!"

THE NEXT MORNING GLENN and I had to report for duty, and we didn't get back out into town until late in the afternoon the next day. We had a rotating duty with the *Starboard Section* of Crash/Fire. 24 hours on, 24 hours off for 4 days, then 48 on and 48 off. It was a truly great duty assignment.

But Flora was gone by then, back to her province in the countryside. We had gone out to her house, which she rented with some other girls, and the *houseboy* Mono, who was at least in his mid-forties, and not a boy, told us Flora had left very early that morning. So, there was nothing we could do. The province, for one thing, was too far away for us to go and still get back in time for work the next morning. Besides, we didn't really want to go. I know I didn't. There was a curfew at night, for one thing. And the Huks. Commie terrorists. They are still around from the old *Huk rebellion* of the 1950s. I guess nowadays there are two kinds of Huks. One group is the original group, the holdover commies, who are all old men now, mainly a bunch of robbers. They ride horses and rob people on the highways. Like cowboys. Then there are the new Huks, real baddies, terrorists. One time, not so long ago, up in a town called San Marcelino, they shot up the Mayor and the whole town council while they sat playing cards in the Mayor's house. With machine guns! And they hate Americans. So, we didn't want to go chasing after Flora.

Besides, what would we be chasing her for? So we could tell her to not get an abortion? That everything was gonna be cool? That Glenn would send her money every month, for the rest of her life? Or until the kid was 18 anyway?

None of those things were true, and I knew it, and so did Glenn. He wasn't going to send her money, not if he could help it, and everything wasn't going to be cool. We knew Flora knew these things too.

We sat in the club where Flora worked. Sat drinking beer and waiting. We waited like every other day for the day to end, for the night to come. Then like any other night, we would sit and drink more beer, listening to the bands playing in the *New Life Club*, letting our minds escape with the music until it was time to beat the curfew, get back on the base, and crash out in our bunks. That is pretty much what we did every day.

But the word does get around. *Old Mama*, who was the *Mama-San* of all the hostesses in the club, came to talk to us. She ambled over, smiling her familiar empty fat smile, and sat uninvited at our table during a music break.

"Hello Mama-San," I said.

Glenn sipped his beer.

Old Mama smiled at me and reached out to clasp my arm on the table with her warm dry hand. There was a sort of pleading look in her eyes, but I couldn't be sure of it. She looked at Glenn, releasing my arm, and he finally grinned at her. "How are you, Mama-San?" he asked cheerfully.

"Okay," she said. "Maybe a little bit tired."

"I guess it's been kind of slow lately," Glenn said.

"Yes, but hopefully a ship will come soon."

"Shangri-La will be in next week."

"Good," said Old Mama, nodding her wide, flat-faced head.

I coughed into my hand.

"Have you talked to Flora?" Glenn asked.

"Oh, yes."

"Did she tell you when she'll come back?"

"It will be a long time."

"Well, I wanted to talk before she left," said Glenn.

"Maybe you send a letter?"

"Hmm. Do you have her address?"

"No, sorry, no address."

"Neither does her houseboy, Mono. Nobody seems to know."

Glenn was silent for a long moment, then said, "Old Mama, did she talk to you before she left town?"

"No," she replied, glancing at me.

"I gotta hit the head," I said, rising to my feet. I hurried back into the stinking toilet to wait there for a full ten minutes, by my watch, before I went back out. Old Mama had left by then.

"Well, what did she tell you?"

"She said a lot of things," Glenn said, looking resigned.

"Okay, like what?"

"She told me what Flora *could* do if she wants to make trouble. I guess Old Mama was trying to be helpful."

"What she *could* do? Okay, please share the bad news."

"After she has the baby, see, she could take me to court. The Philippines court. Mama says here in the PI blood type is considered proof enough. Then the court would do whatever Flora wanted them to do with me."

"What? That's a bunch of bullshit, man." But what did I know?

"Like if she said, let him go, they'd let me go. She could ask for alimony. Child support I mean. Or, she could even tell them to put me in prison. And the Navy would probably go along with it."

"Bullshit," I repeated, not sounding convinced even to myself. "The father could be anybody."

"That," said Glenn, "is why they accept blood type as proof enough. So, guess whose side they'd be on?"

THE WEEKS PASSED BY. Time doesn't pass slowly or quickly when you are stationed in Subic Bay at NAS Cubi Point. It passes both quickly and slowly at the same time. You don't count the days of the week. Instead, you wait for payday. You wait to get off work. You wait for a movie you want to see. You wait for the night, and you wait for Liberty most of all. You try to not think about that day in the distant future when your tour will be up. Every month or so a friend gets shipped out, either for home or another duty station or ship, and you watch him carry his seabag down the steps of the barracks, grinning if he's going home, trying to hide his joy from everyone. Of course, you also get to see all the new guys coming on board, knowing you will be leaving long before they do. And you can't help bullshitting with them:

"When are you shipping out?" some new guy always asks.

"Oh, in exactly 3 months and 12 days."

"So, what's it like here?"

"Fantastic. Sin City's right outside the main gate."

But time passes slowly. Every time a new month comes around it's a great thing, an anniversary of sorts. You celebrate one end by starting the wait for the next one.

I spent most of my Liberty evenings in Olongapo town at the New Life Club, where two great bands took turns playing sets lasting 45 minutes to an hour. The Freedom Highway, and the Black Hawks. I liked both since they played the kind of music I listened to back home, music from groups like Cream, the Beatles and the Stones, and Santana and the Doors. Since the New Life Club wasn't very big, it had a small dance floor, and to me, it felt like a real nightclub back home, where one could really listen to the music. Not that I had gone to that many clubs back home. But it was how I imagined it *could* be, and besides, it passed the time.

Of course, it would have been great if my wife back home could have experienced those nights with me, but I tried not to think about it too much. Well, not while I was out in town drinking, anyway. Back on the base, while on duty out on Hardstand or down at the enlisted beach or in the mess, or laying sleepless and sweaty in my bunk, just about anywhere except out in the town, I would think of home and my old lady. I thought of her all the time. I wrote letters home at least twice a week, but out in the town, everyone seemed too far away to think about. Maybe that's why everyone called the US of A *the world*. It seemed too far away to even be real anymore. I had been here for almost a year, and I was going home on leave in a few months. Man, I didn't want to do anything I would feel guilty about or need lie about, which could be tough.

I went out in town almost every night that I wasn't on duty. And on one of those visits I met a woman named Rosie.

I had a few friends in the other duty section of Crash/Fire, Paul Sutton, and Don Frank. They were from California like me and Glenn, and we'd even gone through basic training with them. And although we hadn't seen each other since boot camp, we'd become good friends. They both surfed too. But being assigned in rotating duty sections meant we never had Liberty on the same days, and so never went out to town together. Nowadays we only saw those guys during morning Quarters, when the duty sections switched.

I had heard Sutton had a new girlfriend in town, supposedly a real knock-out who worked in the Sherry Club. I'd heard she was new in town, having come here from Manila with her sister. *Manila girls*, some called them. But I usually didn't go into the Sherry Club and had pretty much forgotten about Sutton and this woman he had fallen for. Until that evening when Mama-San brought her over to introduce me.

It was dark in the back corner of the club, my usual table, and Glenn wasn't there. I was alone, drinking my second San Miguel beer, the bands hadn't started playing yet, and this was a dingy dank smelly nightclub. But I suddenly found myself standing up like a gentleman to meet this tall woman in front of me.

"Little Eddie, this is Rosie. She will be working here now, I hope you will be nice to her." Old Mama was grinning hugely.

Being nice only meant buying the lady a few drinks and letting her get your beers from the bar instead of getting them yourself. I knew how it worked. I stammered out some sort of words to Old Mama, and then I was sitting there with one of the most beautiful Filipinas I had ever seen. And that's saying something really, because during my ten months, I had hit almost every club in town, both day and night, and there were lots of beautiful women. I'm not sure what it was really, about her I mean. She had a certain *quality,* I suppose. There were many, many girls with long black hair and pretty smiles. They were almost everywhere you looked.

But she had an aura about her, I guess. Every guy stared whenever she entered a room.

"I know who you are," she told me. She smiled warmly, a very genuine kind of smile. Her eyes never left mine.

"Uh, okay. Wow. I mean, okay, it's a small club." I didn't have a clue what else to say.

"Oh, but I know Flora," she said.

"Oh, I get it now! You're here to take her place until she can come back!"

Rosie smiled. "Yes, and I know where you and Glenn work."

"Oh yeah, huh? That's cool. We're in..."

"Crash/Fire crew. Yes, same as my boyfriend, Paul Sutton!"

TWO MONTHS PASSED BEFORE Flora returned to Olongapo City. I went out into town a little late that day since it was payday. I had to visit the Exchange, so Glenn went ahead of me. He was supposed to wait for me at Kong's restaurant, but he wasn't there, so I went across the street to ask Old Mama-San if she had seen him.

"He go to hospital."

"What? Why?" I was surprised I suppose, but not shocked.

"To visit Flora." She smiled.

"Uh, what room is she in?"

"No room, go to Ward Seven."

I caught a cab out to the big hospital off of Rizal Avenue. It wasn't too far, but I didn't trust a jeepney for this ride. I went inside, asking at Reception where Ward Seven was. I got a few different answers, then finally, found it on the second floor.

But Glenn wasn't there. Flora lay in a bed looking very pale, and older than she was. I smiled my best smile.

"What you want?" she asked, pulling her sheet up high under her chin.

"What happened?" I asked stupidly.

"What you mean, what happen? Are you blind?"

"Flora, please."

"Okay. I lose baby. So what?"

"I'm sorry," I said.

"Why? No big deal."

"Well, I'm sorry anyway. Has Glenn been here?"

"Oh yes, he was here. I think he very happy now."

"I don't know," I said. "You could be wrong about that."

She didn't say anything, but turned on her side in the bed, facing away from me. Then a nurse came into the room to shoo me away.

I left her to look for my friend, thinking that now it was over, he could maybe at least *pretend* to be sorry. It was his kid too, and he ought to be sorry, even if I had to ram it down his throat. Flora was a loser I supposed, and might always be a loser, but why rub that in her face? She might have died! I felt like I had to talk to Glenn.

I found him in Ding's Club, drinking cherry brandy and Seven Up on ice, sitting in his favorite corner listening to his favorite music on the jukebox. Since he was sitting right next to the jukebox, I had to wait for the music to end before I could speak.

"I saw Flora," I said, my voice sounding loud in the sudden quiet.

"Yeah?"

"Yeah."

"Looked terrible, didn't she?" he asked lightly.

"Yeah, I guess." What an ass he can be, I thought.

"Well, what'd she tell you?" asked Glenn. He had a funny look on his face like he was beginning to see I was angry with him.

It caught me off guard a bit. "Huh? Well, you know..."

"No, I don't know."

"What's that supposed to mean?"

Glenn looked me in the eye. "Whatever she told you, she didn't lose that baby. She aborted it. The doctor stood right there and told me so, right in front of her."

"What? I didn't think she'd do that." Nothing was making any sense.

"It's true. And she had to admit it."

"But why would she lie? And why did she wait so long?"

"I think she's playing games again," said Glenn.

"It doesn't make sense," I said.

"Yeah, these broads never make sense."

I nodded dumbly. Maybe it wasn't Glenn's baby after all. That was the only explanation that made any sense to me.

"But it was my kid," said Glenn, pouring himself another drink.

"You want a smoke?" I asked.

IT TOOK A WHILE TO finally get to the truth of the thing. Mama-San explained it this way:

"Flora couldn't have baby. She would die. She got too sick, too much pain, so her parents took her to hospital. To save her life."

"But Mama, Glenn says the Doctor told him the story in front of her, right in front of Flora." I looked at Rosie, who was sitting with us there in the late afternoon.

"No," said Rosie, watching me intently.

Mama-San shrugged.

There had been complications, and Flora had chosen to end the pregnancy. Rosie explained everything; The complications were life-threatening, and the baby was unlikely to have lived anyway. There hadn't been time to find Glenn, and besides, he didn't seem willing to admit it was his child. Flora would recover fully. I wasn't sure their relationship would, but I knew I would try to help them.

AND ROSIE HELPED ME. She asked me to bring Drifty to the club and took turns dancing with us, making him laugh and smile. But she didn't flirt, not the way the other girls might have done. Well, she knew I was married and even kept bugging me to show her pictures of my wife back home. She had rules about married men, she told us flatly. So, she wasn't flirting when she sat with us, and the only time we saw her working her trade was when a ship was in and there were sailors in uniform in the club. With us, she was only a friend. Maybe a little lonely, but just a friend. She treated Glenn the same as well, ignoring his repeated declarations that he and Flora were finished. "No," she told him. "She will come back, and you will be with her. Because she needs you, and you need her."

Glenn gave up arguing, since both Rosie, her sister Margaret, and even the Mama-San had told him the truth. And I think he missed her. But stubbornly, he wouldn't say so.

Well, I went Stateside a few weeks later, on 30 days leave. Home to my wife, and my hometown, San Diego. It was summer, and I hadn't been able to go surfing in twelve months, so that was great. It was also the summer that the Woodstock film came out, so overall, it was great to be home, back in *the World*.

Well, I nearly froze surfing in the cold southern California ocean. I had become acclimatized to the warmth of the tropical waters in the PI. So, even though I loved being home, I couldn't wait to get back, although I did my best to hide that from my wife and family.

When I returned to the Philippines, I still had two days of Leave before I had to report back for work. So, for once, I got to go into town and hang out with my old friends Paul Sutton and Don Frank!

It felt a little weird sitting in the club with them and with the beautiful Rosie and her lively sister Mar. It felt a little awkward I guess, but Rosie was friendly, and even asked me to tell them about my trip home, maybe a subtle way of letting Sutton know I was never a threat to him.

And then she announced happily that Glenn and Flora were engaged to be married! What kind of miracle had this woman worked while I'd been in the States? I couldn't help but wonder, and I remember getting chills as my eyes suddenly welled up.

DREAM

The lone lion
Sits in your living room
He's tired and lonely
Seems unconcerned
only looked at me once
making me wonder
just where you'd gone
Such a big cat!
I almost said aloud
As he turned his gaze
Out your wide open window
So, I just sat back
And trying to relax
In your old leather chair
I was thumbing the photos
In that old travel book
Waiting and wondering
When you'd ever return
And turning one last page
What do I see?
A beautiful lioness
Gazing back at me.
She's sitting in the grass
Of some faraway field

and when the lion turns his head
I show him the page
And he licks it just once
Right out of the book.

Thank you!

Please follow me on Goodreads:
https://www.goodreads.com/author/show/18443474.W_B_Edwards